VIOLET STR

# An Intangible Clue

# ANNA KATHARINE GREEN

# PROBLEM 3

first published in 1915

"Not I."

"Not studied the case which for the last few days has provided the papers with such conspicuous headlines?"

"I do not read the papers. I have not looked at one in a whole week."

"Miss Strange, your social engagements

must be of a very pressing nature just now?"

"They are."

"And your business sense in abeyance?"

"How so?"

"You would not ask if you had read the papers."

To this she made no reply save by a slight toss of her

pretty head. If her employer felt nettled by this show of indifference, he did not betray it save by the rapidity of his tones as, without further preamble and possibly without real excuse, he proceeded to lay before her the case in question. "Last Tuesday night a woman was murdered in this city; an old woman, in a lonely house where she has lived for years. Perhaps you remember this house? It occupies a not inconspicuous site in Seventeenth Street—a house of the olden time?"

"No, I do not remember."

The extreme carelessness of Miss Strange's tone would have been fatal to her socially; but then, she would never have used it socially. This they both knew, yet he smiled with his customary indulgence.

"Then I will describe it."

She looked around for a chair and sank into it. He did the same.

"It has a fanlight over the front door."

She remained impassive.

"And two old-fashioned strips of parti-coloured glass on either side."

"And a knocker between its panels which may bring money some day."

"Oh, you do remember! I thought you would, Miss Strange."

"Yes. Fanlights over doors are becoming very rare in New York."

"Very well, then. That house was the scene of Tuesday's tragedy. The woman who has lived there in solitude for years was foully murdered. I have since heard that the people who knew her best have always anticipated some such violent end for her. She never allowed maid or friend to remain with her after five in the afternoon; yet she had money— some think a great deal—always in the house."

"I am interested in the house, not in her."

"Yet, she was a character—as

full of whims and crotchets as a nut is of meat. Her death was horrible. She fought—her dress was torn from her body in rags. This happened, you see, before her hour for retiring; some think as early as six in the afternoon. And"—here he made a rapid gesture to catch Violet's wandering attention—"in spite of this struggle; in spite of the fact that she was dragged from room to room— that her person was searched—and everything in the house searched—that drawers were pulled out of bureaus— doors wrenched off of cupboards— china smashed upon the floor—whole shelves denuded and not a spot from cellar to garret left unransacked, no direct clue to the perpetrator has been found—nothing that gives any idea of his personality save his display of strength and great cupidity. The police have even deigned to consult me,—an unusual procedure—but I could find nothing, either. Evidences of fiendish purpose abound—of relentless search—but no clue to the man himself. It's uncommon, isn't it, not to have any clue?"

"I suppose so." Miss Strange hated murders and it was with difficulty she could be brought to discuss them. But she was not going to be let off; not this time.

"You see,"

he proceeded insistently, "it's not only mortifying to the police but disappointing to the press, especially as few reporters believe in the No-thoroughfare business. They say, and we cannot but agree with them, that no such struggle could take place and no such repeated goings to and fro through the house without some vestige being left by which to connect this crime with its daring perpetrator."

Still she stared down at her hands—those little hands so white and fluttering, so seemingly helpless under the weight of their many rings, and yet so slyly capable.

"She must have

queer neighbours," came at last, from Miss Strange's reluctant lips. "Didn't they hear or see anything of all this?"

"She has no neighbours—that is, after half-past five o'clock. There's a printing establishment on one side of her, a deserted mansion on the other side, and nothing but warehouses back and front. There was no one to notice what took place in her small dwelling after the printing house was closed. She was the most courageous or the most foolish of women to remain there as she did. But nothing except death could budge her. She was born in the room where she died; was married in the one where she worked; saw husband, father, mother, and five sisters carried out in turn to their graves through the door with the fanlight over the top—and these memories held her."

"You are trying to interest me in the woman. Don't."

"No, I'm not trying to interest you in her,

only trying to explain her. There was another reason for her remaining where she did so long after all residents had left the block. She had a business."

"Oh!"

"She embroidered monograms for fine ladies."

"She did? But you needn't look at me

like that. She never embroidered any for me."

"No? She did first-class work. I saw some of it. Miss Strange, if I could get you into that house for ten minutes—not to see her but to pick up the loose intangible thread which I am sure is floating around in it somewhere—wouldn't you go?"

Violet slowly rose—a movement which
he followed to the letter.

"Must I express in words the limit I have set for myself in our affair?" she asked. "When, for reasons I have never thought myself called upon to explain, I consented to help you a little now and then with some matter where a woman's tact and knowledge of the social world might tell without offence to herself or others, I never thought it would be necessary for me to state that temptation must stop with such cases, or that I should not be asked to touch the sordid or the bloody. But it seems I was mistaken, and that

I must stoop to be explicit. The woman who was killed on Tuesday might have interested me greatly as an embroiderer, but as a victim, not at all. What do you see in me, or miss in me, that you should drag me into an atmosphere of low-down crime?"

"Nothing, Miss Strange. You are by

nature, as well as by breeding, very far removed from everything of the kind. But you will allow me to suggest that no crime is low-down which makes imperative demand upon the intellect and intuitive sense of its investigator. Only the most delicate touch can feel and hold the thread I've just spoken of, and you have the most delicate touch I know."

"Do not attempt to flatter me. I have no fancy for handling befouled spider webs. Besides, if I had—if such elusive filaments fascinated me—how could I, well-known in person and name, enter upon such a scene without prejudice to our mutual compact?"

"Miss Strange"—she had reseated herself, but so far he had failed to follow her example (an ignoring of the subtle hint that her interest might yet be caught, which seemed to annoy her a trifle), "I should not even have suggested such a possibility had

I not seen a way of introducing you there without risk to your position or mine. Among the boxes piled upon Mrs. Doolittle's table—boxes of finished work, most of them addressed and ready for delivery—was one on which could be seen the name of—shall I mention it?"

"Not mine? You don't mean mine? That would be too odd—too ridiculously odd. I should not understand a coincidence of that kind; no, I should not, notwithstanding the fact that I have lately sent out such work to be done."

"Yet it was your name, very clearly and precisely

written—your whole name, Miss Strange. I saw and read it myself."

"But I gave the order to Madame Pirot on Fifth Avenue. How came my things to be found in the house of this woman of whose horrible death we have been talking?"

"Did you suppose that Madame Pirot did such work with

her own hands?—
or even had it
done in her own
establishment?
Mrs. Doolittle was
universally employed.
She worked for a
dozen firms. You
will find the biggest
names on most of
her packages. But on
this one—I allude to
the one addressed to
you—there was more
to be seen than the
name. These words

were written on it in another hand. Send without opening. This struck the police as suspicious; sufficiently so, at least, for them to desire your presence at the house as soon as you can make it convenient."

"To open the box?"

"Exactly."

The curl of Miss

Strange's disdainful lip was a sight to see.

"You wrote those words yourself," she coolly observed. "While someone's back was turned, you whipped out your pencil and—"

"Resorted to a very pardonable subterfuge highly conducive to the public's good. But never mind that. Will you go?"

Miss Strange became suddenly demure.

"I suppose I must," she grudgingly conceded. "However obtained, a summons from the police cannot be ignored even by Peter Strange's daughter."

Another man might have displayed his triumph by smile or

gesture; but this one had learned his role too well. He simply said:

"Very good. Shall it be at once? I have a taxi at the door."

But she failed to see the necessity of any such hurry. With sudden dignity she replied:

"That won't do. If I go to this house

it must be under
suitable conditions.
I shall have to
ask my brother to
accompany me."

"Your brother!"

"Oh, he's safe. He—
he knows."

"Your brother
knows?" Her visitor,
with less control
than usual, betrayed
very openly his
uneasiness.

"He does and—approves. But that's not what interests us now, only so far as it makes it possible for me to go with propriety to that dreadful house."

A formal bow from the other and the words:

"They may expect you, then. Can you say when?"

"Within the next hour. But it will be a useless concession on my part," she pettishly complained. "A place that has been gone over by a dozen detectives is apt to be brushed clean of its cobwebs, even if such ever existed."

"That's the difficulty," he acknowledged; and

did not dare to add another word; she was at that particular moment so very much the great lady, and so little his confidential agent.

He might have been less impressed, however, by this sudden assumption of manner, had he been so fortunate as to have seen how she employed the three quarters of an hour's delay for which she had asked.

She read those neglected newspapers, especially the one containing the following highly coloured narration of this ghastly crime:

"A door ajar—an empty hall—a line of sinister looking blotches marking a guilty step diagonally across the flagging—silence—and an unmistakable odour repugnant to all humanity,—such were the indications which met the eyes of Officer O'Leary on his first round last night, and led to the discovery of a murder which will long thrill the city by its mystery and horror.

"Both the house and the victim are well known." Here followed a description of the same and of Mrs. Doolittle's manner of life in her ancient home, which Violet hurriedly passed over to come to the following:

"As far as one can judge from appearances, the

crime happened in this wise: Mrs. Doolittle had been in her kitchen, as the tea-kettle found singing on the stove goes to prove, and was coming back through her bedroom, when the wretch, who had stolen in by the front door which, to save steps, she was unfortunately in the habit of leaving on the latch till all possibility of customers for the day was over, sprang upon her from behind and dealt her a swinging blow with the poker he had caught up from the hearthstone.

"Whether the struggle which ensued followed immediately upon this first attack or came later, it will take medical experts to determine. But, whenever it did occur, the fierceness of its character is shown by the grip taken upon her throat and the traces of blood which are to be seen all over the house. If the wretch had lugged her into her workroom and thence to the kitchen, and thence back to the spot of first assault, the evidences could not have been more ghastly. Bits of her clothing torn off by a ruthless hand, lay scattered over all these floors. In her bedroom, where she finally breathed her last, there could be seen mingled with these a number of large but worthless glass beads; and close against one of the base-boards, the string which had held them, as shown by the few remaining beads still clinging to it. If in pulling the string from her neck he had hoped to light upon some valuable booty, his fury at his disappointment is evident. You can almost see the frenzy with which he flung the would-be necklace at the wall, and kicked about and stamped upon its rapidly rolling beads.

"Booty! That was what he was after; to find and carry away the poor needlewoman's supposed hoardings. If the scene baffles description—if, as some believe, he dragged her yet living from spot to spot, demanding information as to her places of concealment under threat of repeated blows, and, finally baffled, dealt the finishing stroke and proceeded on the search alone, no greater devastation could have taken place in this poor woman's house or effects. Yet such was his precaution and care for himself that he left no finger-print behind him nor any other token which could lead to personal identification. Even though his footsteps could be traced in much the order I have mentioned, they were of so indeterminate and shapeless a character as to convey little to the intelligence of the investigator.

"That these smears (they could not be called footprints) not only crossed the hall but appeared in more than one place on the staircase proves that he did not confine his search to the lower storey; and perhaps one of the most interesting features of the case lies in the indications given by these marks of the raging course he took through these upper rooms. As the accompanying diagram will show [we omit the diagram] he went first into the large front chamber, thence to the rear where we find two rooms, one unfinished and filled with accumulated stuff most of which he left lying loose upon the floor, and the other plastered, and containing a window opening upon an alley-way at the side, but empty of all furniture and without even a carpet on the bare boards.

"Why he should have entered the latter place, and why, having entered he should have crossed to the window, will be plain to those who have studied

the conditions.
The front chamber
windows were tightly
shuttered, the attic
ones cumbered with
boxes and shielded
from approach by
old bureaus and
discarded chairs.
This one only was
free and, although
darkened by the
proximity of the
house neighbouring
it across the alley,
was the only spot

on the storey where
sufficient light
could be had at this
late hour for the
examination of any
object of whose value
he was doubtful.
That he had come
across such an object
and had brought it
to this window for
some such purpose
is very satisfactorily
demonstrated by the
discovery of a worn
out wallet of ancient

make lying on the floor directly in front of this window—a proof of his cupidity but also proof of his ill-luck. For this wallet, when lifted and opened, was found to contain two hundred or more dollars in old bills, which, if not the full hoard of their industrious owner, was certainly worth the taking by one who had risked his neck for the sole purpose of theft.

"This wallet, and the flight of the murderer without it, give to this affair, otherwise simply brutal, a dramatic interest which will be appreciated not only by the very able detectives already hot upon the chase, but by all other inquiring minds anxious to solve a mystery of which so estimable a woman has been the unfortunate victim. A problem is presented to the police—"

There Violet stopped.

When, not long after, the superb limousine of Peter Strange stopped before the little house in Seventeenth Street, it caused a veritable sensation, not only in the curiosity-mongers lingering on the sidewalk, but to the two persons within—the officer on guard and a belated reporter.

Though dressed in her plainest suit, Violet Strange looked much too fashionable and far too young and thoughtless to be observed, without emotion, entering a scene of hideous and brutal crime. Even the young man who accompanied her promised to bring a most incongruous element into this atmosphere of guilt and horror, and, as the detective on guard whispered to the man beside him, might much better have been left behind in the car.

But Violet was great for the proprieties and young Arthur followed her in.

Her entrance was a coup du theatre. She had lifted her veil in crossing the sidewalk and her interesting features and general air of timidity were very fetching. As the man holding open the door noted the impression made upon his companion, he muttered with sly facetiousness:

"You think you'll show her nothing; but I'm ready to bet a fiver that she'll want to see it all and that you'll show it to her."

The detective's grin was expressive, notwithstanding the shrug with which he tried to carry it off.

And Violet? The hall into which she now stepped from the most vivid sunlight had never been considered even in its palmiest days as possessing cheer even of the stately kind. The ghastly green light infused through it by the coloured glass on either side of the doorway seemed to promise yet more dismal things beyond.

"Must I go in there?" she asked, pointing, with an admirable simulation of nervous excitement, to a half-shut door at her left. "Is there where it happened? Arthur, do you suppose that there is where it happened?"

"No, no, Miss," the officer made haste to assure her. "If you

are Miss Strange"
(Violet bowed), "I
need hardly say
that the woman
was struck in her
bedroom. The door
beside you leads into
the parlour, or as she
would have called it,
her work-room. You
needn't be afraid of
going in there. You
will see nothing but
the disorder of her
boxes. They were
pretty well pulled

about. Not all of them though," he added, watching her as closely as the dim light permitted. "There is one which gives no sign of having been tampered with. It was done up in wrapping paper and is addressed to you, which in itself would not have seemed worthy of our attention had not these lines been scribbled on it in a man's handwriting: 'Send without opening.'"

"How odd!" exclaimed the little minx with widely opened eyes and an air of guileless innocence. "Whatever can it mean? Nothing serious I am sure, for the woman did not even know me. She was employed to do this work by Madame Pirot."

"Didn't you know that it was to be done here?"

"No. I thought Madame Pirot's own girls did her embroidery for her."

"So that you were surprised—"

"Wasn't I!"

"To get our

message."

"I didn't know what to make of it."

The earnest, half-injured look with which she uttered this disclaimer, did its appointed work. The detective accepted her for what she seemed and, oblivious to the reporter's satirical gesture, crossed to the work-room door, which he threw wide open with the remark:

"I should be glad to have you open that box in our presence. It is undoubtedly all right, but we wish to be sure. You know what the box should contain?"

"Oh, yes, indeed; pillow-cases and sheets, with a big S embroidered on them."

"Very well. Shall I undo the string for you?"

"I shall be much obliged," said she, her eye flashing quickly about the room before settling down upon the knot he was deftly loosening.

Her brother, gazing indifferently in from

the doorway, hardly noticed this look; but the reporter at his back did, though he failed to detect its penetrating quality.

"Your name is on the other side," observed the detective as he drew away the string and turned the package over.

The smile which just lifted the corner of her lips

was not in answer to this remark, but to her recognition of her employer's handwriting in the words under her name: Send without opening. She had not misjudged him.

"The cover you may like to take off yourself," suggested the officer, as he lifted the box out of its wrapper.

"Oh, I don't mind. There's nothing to be ashamed of in embroidered linen. Or perhaps that is not what you are looking for?"

No one answered. All were busy watching her whip off the lid and lift out the pile of sheets and pillow-cases with which the box was closely packed.

"Shall I unfold them?" she asked.

The detective nodded.

Taking out the topmost sheet, she shook it open. Then the next and the next till she reached the bottom of the box. Nothing of a criminating nature came to light. The box as well as its contents was without mystery of any kind. This was not an unexpected result of course, but the smile with which she began to refold the pieces and throw them back into the box, revealed one of her dimples which was almost as dangerous to the casual observer as when it revealed both.

"There," she

exclaimed, "you see! Household linen exactly as I said. Now may I go home?"

"Certainly, Miss Strange."

The detective stole a sly glance at the reporter. She was not going in for the horrors then after all.

But the reporter abated nothing of his knowing air, for

while she spoke of going, she made no move towards doing so, but continued to look about the room till her glances finally settled on a long dark curtain shutting off an adjoining room.

"There's where she lies, I suppose," she feelingly exclaimed. "And not one of you knows who killed her.

Somehow, I cannot understand that. Why don't you know when that's what you're hired for?" The innocence with which she uttered this was astonishing. The detective began to look sheepish and the reporter turned aside to hide his smile. Whether in another moment either would have spoken no one can say, for, with a mock consciousness of having said something foolish, she caught up her parasol from the table and made a start for the door.

But of course she looked back.

"I was wondering," she recommenced, with a half wistful, half speculative air, "whether I should ask to have a peep at the place where it all happened."

The reporter chuckled behind the pencil-end he was chewing, but the officer maintained his solemn air, for which act of self-restraint he was undoubtedly grateful when in another minute she gave a quick impulsive shudder not altogether assumed, and vehemently added: "But I couldn't stand the sight; no, I couldn't! I'm an awful coward when it comes to things like that. Nothing in all the world would induce me to look at the woman or her room. But I should like—" here both her dimples came into play though she could not be said exactly to smile—"just one little look upstairs, where he went poking about so long without any fear it seems of being interrupted. Ever since I've read about it I have seen, in my mind, a picture of his wicked figure sneaking from room to room, tearing open drawers and flinging out the contents of closets just to find a little money—a little, little money! I shall not sleep to-night just for wondering how those high up attic rooms really look."

Who could dream that back of this display of mingled childishness and audacity there lay hidden purpose, intellect, and a keen knowledge of human nature. Not the two men who listened to this seemingly irresponsible chatter. To them she was a child to be humoured and humour her they did. The dainty feet which had already found their way to that gloomy staircase were allowed to ascend, followed it is true by those of the officer who did not dare to smile back at the reporter because of the brother's watchful and none too conciliatory eye.

At the stair head she paused to look back.

"I don't see those horrible marks which the papers describe as running all along the lower hall and up these stairs."

"No, Miss Strange; they have gradually been rubbed out, but you will find some still showing on these upper floors."

"Oh! oh! where? You frighten me—frighten me horribly! But—but—if you don't mind, I should like to see."

Why should not a man on a tedious job amuse himself? Piloting her over to the small room in the rear, he pointed down at the boards.

She gave one look and then stepped gingerly in.

"Just look!" she cried; "a whole string of marks going straight from door to window. They have no shape, have they,—just blotches? I wonder why one of them is so much larger than the rest?"

This was no new question. It was one

which everybody who went into the room was sure to ask, there was such a difference in the size and appearance of the mark nearest the window. The reason—well, minds were divided about that, and no one had a satisfactory theory. The detective therefore kept discreetly silent.

This did not seem to offend Miss Strange. On the contrary it gave her an opportunity to babble away to her heart's content.

"One, two, three, four, five, six," she counted, with a shudder at every count. "And one of them bigger than the others." She might have added,

"It is the trail of one foot, and strangely, intermingled at that," but she did not, though we may be quite sure that she noted the fact. "And where, just where did the old wallet fall? Here? or here?"

She had moved as she spoke, so that in uttering the last "here," she stood directly before the window. The surprise she received there nearly made her forget the part she was playing. From the character of the light in the room, she had expected, on looking out, to confront a near-by wall, but not a window in that wall. Yet that was what she saw directly facing her from across the old-fashioned alley separating this house from its neighbour; twelve unshuttered and uncurtained panes through which she caught a darkened view of a room almost as forlorn and devoid of furniture as the one in which she then stood.

When quite sure of herself, she let a certain portion of her surprise appear.

"Why, look!" she cried, "if you can't see right in next door! What a lonesome-looking place! From its desolate appearance I should think the house quite empty."

"And it is. That's the old Shaffer homestead. It's been empty for a year."

"Oh, empty!" And she turned away, with the most inconsequent air in the world, crying out as her name rang up the stair, "There's Arthur calling. I suppose he thinks I've been here long enough. I'm sure I'm very much obliged to you, officer. I really shouldn't have slept a wink to-night, if I hadn't been given a peep at these rooms, which I had imagined so different." And with one additional glance over her shoulder, that seemed to penetrate both windows and the desolate space beyond, she ran quickly out and down in response to her brother's reiterated call.

"Drive quickly!—as

quickly as the law allows, to Hiram Brown's office in Duane Street."

Arrived at the address named, she went in alone to see Mr. Brown. He was her father's lawyer and a family friend.

Hardly waiting for his affectionate greeting, she cried out quickly. "Tell me how I can learn anything about the old Shaffer house in Seventeenth Street. Now, don't look so surprised. I have very good reasons for my request and—and—I'm in an awful hurry."

"But—"

"I know, I know; there's been a dreadful tragedy next door to it; but it's about the Shaffer house itself I want some information. Has it an agent, a—"

"Of course it has an agent, and here is his name."

Mr. Brown presented her with a card on which he had hastily written both name and address.

She thanked him, dropped him a mocking curtsey full

of charm, whispered "Don't tell father," and was gone.

Her manner to the man she next interviewed was very different. As soon as she saw him she subsided into her usual society manner. With just a touch of the conceit of the successful debutante, she announced herself as Miss

Strange of Seventy-second Street. Her business with him was in regard to the possible renting of the Shaffer house. She had an old lady friend who was desirous of living downtown.

In passing through Seventeenth Street, she had noticed that the old Shaffer house was standing empty and had been immediately struck with the advantages it possessed for her elderly friend's occupancy. Could it be that the house was for rent? There was no sign on it to that effect, but—etc.

His answer left her nothing to hope for.

"It is going to be torn down," he said.

"Oh, what a pity!" she exclaimed. "Real colonial, isn't it! I wish I could see the rooms inside before it is disturbed. Such doors and such dear old-fashioned mantelpieces as it must have! I just dote on the Colonial. It brings up such pictures of the old days; weddings, you know, and parties;— all so different from ours and so much more interesting."

Is it the chance shot that tells? Sometimes. Violet had no especial intention in what she said save as a prelude to a pending request, but nothing could have served her purpose better than that one word, wedding. The agent laughed and giving her his first indulgent look, remarked genially:

"Romance is not confined to those ancient times. If you were to enter that house to-day you would come across evidences of a wedding as romantic as any which ever took place in all the seventy odd years of its existence. A man and a woman were married there day before yesterday who did their first courting under its roof forty years ago. He has been married twice and she once in the interval; but the old love held firm and now at the age of sixty and over they have come together to finish their days in peace and happiness. Or so we will hope."

"Married! married in that house and on the day that—"

She caught herself up in time. He did not notice the break.

"Yes, in memory of those old days of courtship, I suppose. They came here about five, got the keys, drove off, went through the ceremony in that empty house, returned the keys to me in my own apartment, took the steamer for Naples, and were on the sea before midnight. Do you not call that quick work as well as highly romantic?"

"Very." Miss Strange's cheek had paled. It was apt to when she was greatly excited. "But I don't understand," she added, the moment after. "How could they do this and nobody know about it? I should have thought it would have got into the papers."

"They are quiet people. I don't think they told their best friends. A simple announcement in the next day's journals testified to the fact of their marriage, but that was all. I would not have felt at liberty to mention the circumstances myself, if the parties were not well on their way to Europe."

"Oh, how glad I am that you did tell me! Such a story of constancy and the hold which old associations have upon sensitive minds! But—"

"Why, Miss? What's the matter? You look very much disturbed."

"Don't you remember? Haven't you thought? Something else happened that very day and almost at the same time on that block. Something very dreadful—"

"Mrs. Doolittle's murder?"

"Yes. It was as near as next door, wasn't it? Oh, if this happy couple had known—"

"But fortunately they didn't. Nor are they likely to, till they reach the other side. You needn't fear that their honeymoon will be spoiled that way."

"But they may have heard something or seen something before leaving the street. Did you notice how the gentleman looked when he returned you the keys?"

"I did, and there was no cloud on his satisfaction."

"Oh, how you relieve me!" One—two dimples made their appearance in Miss Strange's fresh, young cheeks. "Well! I wish them joy. Do you mind telling me their names? I cannot think of them as actual persons without knowing their names."

"The gentleman was Constantin Amidon; the lady, Marian Shaffer. You will have to think of them now as Mr. and Mrs. Amidon."

"And I will. Thank you, Mr. Hutton,

thank you very much. Next to the pleasure of getting the house for my friend, is that of hearing this charming bit of news its connection."

She held out her hand and, as he took it, remarked:

"They must have had a clergyman and witnesses."

"Undoubtedly."

"I wish I had been one of the witnesses," she sighed sentimentally.

"They were two old men."

"Oh, no! Don't tell me that."

"Fogies; nothing less."

"But the clergyman? He must have been young. Surely

there was some one there capable of appreciating the situation?"

"I can't say about that; I did not see the clergyman."

"Oh, well! it doesn't matter." Miss Strange's manner was as nonchalant as it was charming. "We will think of him as being very young."

And with a merry toss of her head she flitted away.

But she sobered very rapidly upon entering her limousine.

"Hello!"

"Ah, is that you?"

"Yes, I want a Marconi sent."

"A Marconi?"

"Yes, to the Cretic,

which left dock the very night in which we are so deeply interested."

"Good. Whom to? The Captain?"

"No, to a Mrs. Constantin Amidon. But first be sure there is such a passenger."

"Mrs.! What idea have you there?"

"Excuse my not stating over the telephone. The message is to be to this effect. Did she at any time immediately before or after her marriage to Mr. Amidon get a glimpse of any one in the adjoining house? No remarks, please. I use the telephone because I am not ready to explain myself. If she did, let her send a written description to you of that person as soon as she reaches the Azores."

"You surprise me. May I not call or hope for a line from you early to-morrow?"

"I shall be busy till you get your answer."

He hung up the receiver. He recognized the

resolute tone.

But the time came when the pending explanation was fully given to him. An answer had been returned from the steamer, favourable to Violet's hopes. Mrs. Amidon had seen such a person and would send a full description of the same at the first opportunity. It was news to fill Violet's heart with pride; the filament of a clue which had led to this great result had been so nearly invisible and had felt so like nothing in her grasp.

To her employer she described it as follows:

"When I hear or read of a case which contains any baffling features, I am apt to feel some hidden chord in my nature thrill to one fact in it and not to any of the others. In this case the single fact which appealed to my imagination was the dropping of the stolen wallet in that upstairs room. Why did the guilty man drop it? and why, having dropped it, did he not pick it up again?

but one answer seemed possible. He had heard or seen something at the spot where it fell which not only alarmed him but sent him in flight from the house."

"Very good; and did you settle to your own mind the nature of that sound or that sight?"

"I did." Her manner was strangely

businesslike. No show of dimples now. "Satisfied that if any possibility remained of my ever doing this, it would have to be on the exact place of this occurrence or not at all, I embraced your suggestion and visited the house."

"And that room no doubt."

"And that room. Women, somehow,

seem to manage such things."

"So I've noticed, Miss Strange. And what was the result of your visit? What did you discover there?"

"This: that one of the blood spots marking the criminal's steps through the room was decidedly more pronounced than the rest; and, what was even more important, that the window out of which I was looking had its counterpart in the house on the opposite side of the alley. In gazing through the one I was gazing through the other; and not only that, but into the darkened area of the room beyond. Instantly I saw how the latter fact might be made to explain the former one. But before I say how, let me ask if it is quite settled among you that the smears on the floor and stairs mark the passage of the criminal's footsteps!"

"Certainly; and very bloody feet they must have been too. His shoes—or rather his one shoe—for the proof is plain

that only the right
one left its mark—
must have become
thoroughly saturated
to carry its traces so
far."

"Do you think that
any amount of
saturation would
have done this? Or,
if you are not ready
to agree to that, that
a shoe so covered
with blood could have
failed to leave behind

it some hint of its shape, some imprint, however faint, of heel or toe? But nowhere did it do this. We see a smear—and that is all."

"You are right, Miss Strange; you are always right. And what do you gather from this?"

She looked to see how much he expected from her,

and, meeting an eye not quite as free from ironic suggestion as his words had led her to expect, faltered a little as she proceeded to say:

"My opinion is a girl's opinion, but such as it is you have the right to have it. From the indications mentioned I could draw but this conclusion: that the blood which accompanied the criminal's footsteps was not carried through the house by his shoes;—he wore no shoes; he did not even wear stockings; probably he had none. For reasons which appealed to his judgment, he went about his wicked work barefoot; and it was the blood from his own veins and not from those of his victim which made the trail we have followed with so much interest. Do you forget those broken beads;—how he kicked them about and stamped upon them in his fury? One of them pierced the ball of his foot, and that so sharply that it not only spurted blood but kept on bleeding with every step he took. Otherwise, the trail would have been lost after his passage up the stairs."

"Fine!" There was no irony in the bureau-chief's eye now. "You are progressing, Miss Strange. Allow me, I pray, to kiss your hand. It is a liberty I have never taken, but one which would greatly relieve my present stress of feeling."

She lifted her hand toward him, but it was in gesture, not in recognition of his homage.

"Thank you," said she, "but I claim no monopoly on deductions so simple as these. I have not the least doubt that not only yourself but every member of the force has made the same. But there is a little matter which may have escaped the police, may even have escaped you. To that I would now call your attention since through it I have been enabled, after a little necessary groping, to reach the open. You remember the one large blotch on the upper floor where the man dropped the wallet? That blotch, more or less commingled with a fainter one, possessed great significance for me from the first moment I saw it. How came his foot to bleed so much more profusely at that one spot than at any other? There could be but one answer: because here a surprise met him—a surprise so startling to him in his present state of mind, that he gave a quick spring backward, with the result that his wounded foot came down suddenly and forcibly instead of easily as in his previous wary tread. And what was the surprise? I made it my business to find out, and now I can tell you that it was the sight of a woman's face staring upon him from the neighbouring house which he had probably been told was empty. The shock disturbed his judgment. He saw his crime discovered— his guilty secret read, and fled in unreasoning panic. He might better have held on to his wits. It was this display of fear which led me to search after its cause, and consequently to discover that at this especial hour more than one person had been in the Shaffer house; that, in fact, a marriage had been celebrated there under circumstances as romantic as any we read of in books, and that this marriage, privately carried out, had been followed by an immediate voyage of the happy couple on one of the White Star steamers. With the rest you are conversant. I do not need to say anything about what has followed the sending of that Marconi."

"But I am going to say something about

your work in this matter, Miss Strange. The big detectives about here will have to look sharp if—"

"Don't, please! Not yet." A smile softened the asperity of this interruption. "The man has yet to be caught and identified. Till that is done I cannot enjoy any one's congratulations. And

you will see that
all this may not be
so easy. If no one
happened to meet
the desperate wretch
before he had an
opportunity to retie
his shoe-laces, there
will be little for
you or even for the
police to go upon but
his wounded foot, his
undoubtedly carefully
prepared alibi, and
later, a woman's
confused description

of a face seen but for a moment only and that under a personal excitement precluding minute attention. I should not be surprised if the whole thing came to nothing."

But it did not. As soon as the description was received from Mrs. Amidon (a description, by the

way, which was
unusually clear
and precise, owing
to the peculiar
and contradictory
features of the man),
the police were able
to recognize him
among the many
suspects always
under their eye.
Arrested, he pleaded,
just as Miss Strange
had foretold, an
alibi of a seemingly
unimpeachable

character; but neither it, nor the plausible explanation with which he endeavoured to account for a freshly healed scar amid the callouses of his right foot, could stand before Mrs. Amidon's unequivocal testimony that he was the same man she had seen in Mrs. Doolittle's upper room on the afternoon of her own happiness and of that poor woman's murder.

The moment when, at his trial, the two faces again confronted each other across a space no wider than that which had separated them on the dread occasion in Seventeenth Street, is said to have been one of the most dramatic in the annals of that ancient court room.

## ABOUT THE AUTHOR

In 1887, a decade before Sherlock Holmes, Anna Katharine Green wrote her first detective story and began her genre defining career. Born in Brooklyn in 1846, she defied a male dominated field and pioneered many conventions of mysteries that remain today.

## ABOUT THE COVER

The image on the cover is adapted from a lithograph by the Austrian-Czech artist Alphonse Mucha entitled, "Flirt". It was made sometime between 1895-1900.

## VIOLET STRANGE RETURNS IN THE GROTTO SPECTRE

# MORE BOOKS AT:

# superlargeprint.com

# KEEP ON READING!

ISBN 9781088950920

Printed by Amazon Italia Logistica S.r.l.
Torrazza Piemonte (TO), Italy

11660739R00089